Stephen W. Martin *and* Juan Carlos Solon

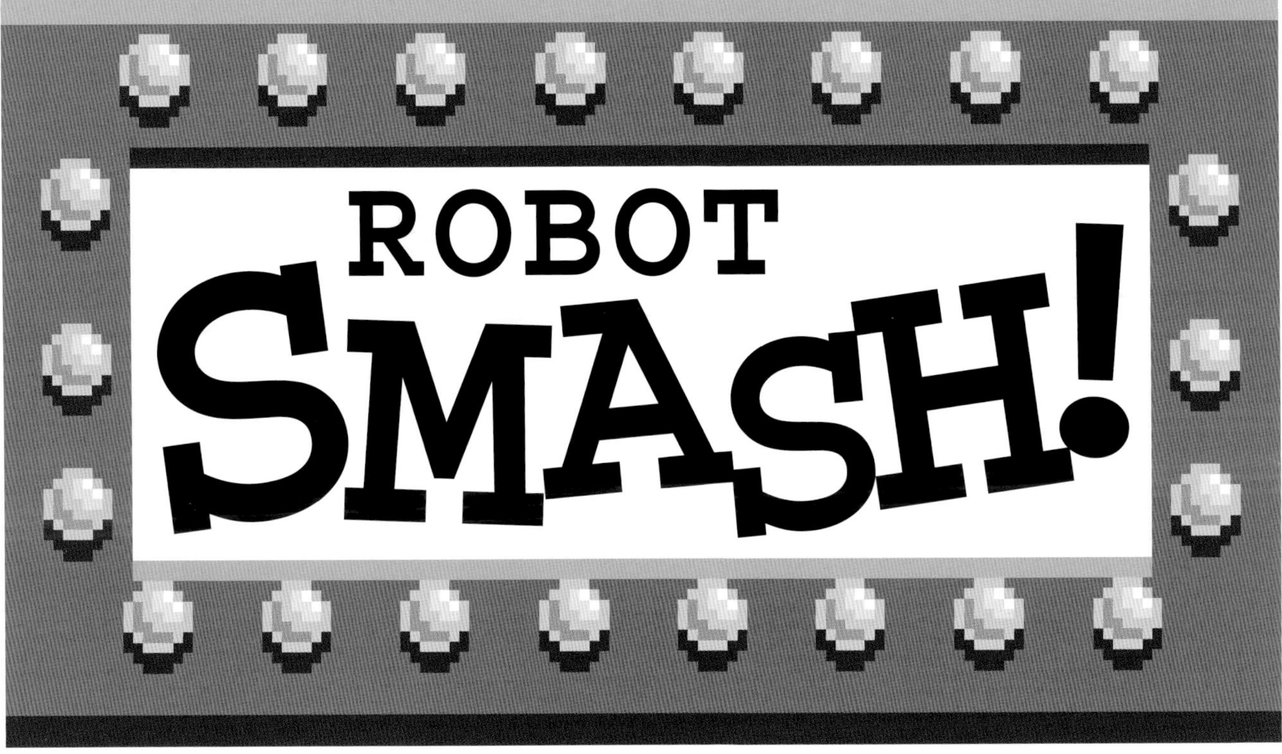

Owlkids Books

For Lola: 011011000110111101110110011001010010
0000011110010110111101110101 – S.M.

To my family for their support. To Charm for her love. To Belle, Blake, Callie, Hannah, Brantley & JJ for keeping me inspired – J.C.S.

Owlkids Books acknowledges the financial support of the Canada Council for the Arts, the Ontario Arts Council, the Government of Canada through the Canada Book Fund (CBF) and the Government of Ontario through the Ontario Media Development Corporation's Book Initiative for our publishing activities.

Published in Canada by
Owlkids Books Inc.
10 Lower Spadina Avenue
Toronto, ON M5V 2Z2

Published in the United States by
Owlkids Books Inc.
1700 Fourth Street
Berkeley, CA 94710

Library and Archives Canada Cataloguing in Publication

Martin, Stephen W., 1981-, author
Robot smash! / written by Stephen W. Martin ; illustrated by Juan Carlos Solon.

ISBN 978-1-77147-067-4 (bound)

I. Solon, Juan Carlos, illustrator II. Title.

PS8626.A77294R62 2015 jC813'.6 C2014-905502-1

Library of Congress Control Number: 2014948888

Edited by: Karen Li
Designed by: Alisa Baldwin

Manufactured in Dongguan, China, in October 2014, by Toppan Leefung Packaging & Printing (Dongguan) Co., Ltd.
Job #BAYDC12

A B C D E F

Publisher of Chirp, chickaDEE and OWL
www.owlkidsbooks.com

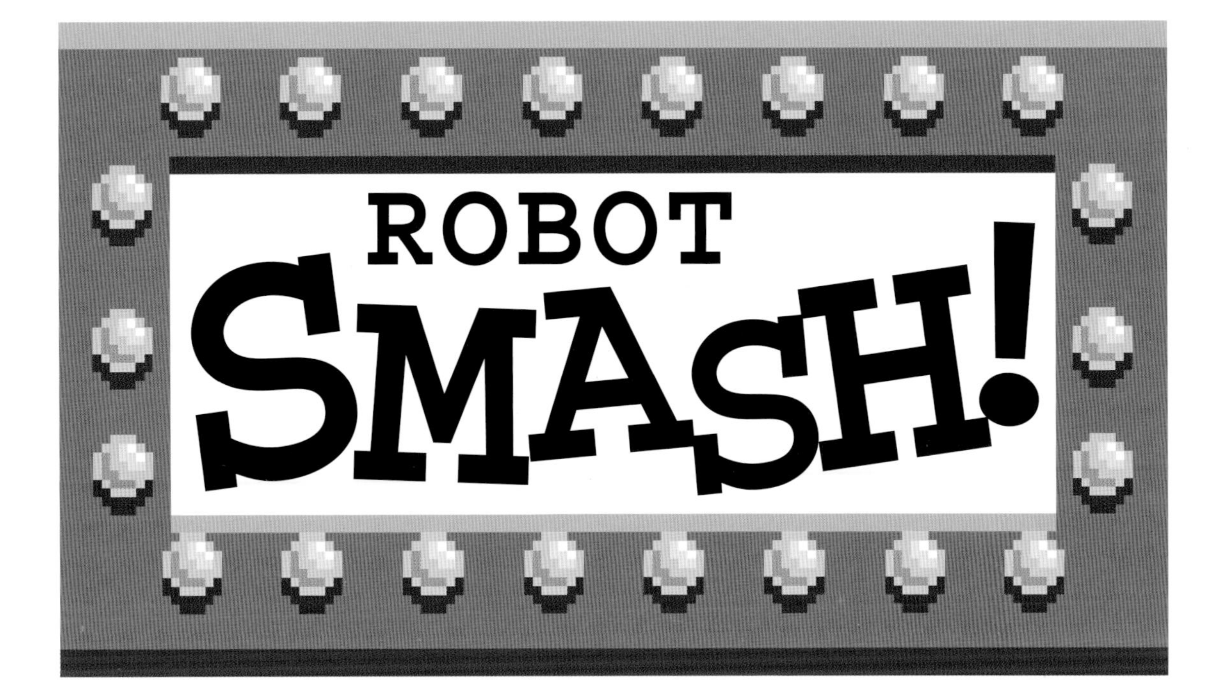

I am a robot.
I like to...

SMASH!

Soda cans...

SMASH!

Petunias...
SMASH!

Toilets...

SMASH!

Garbage trucks... **SMASH!**

Brussels sprouts...
SMASH!

Robot puppy dogs...
SMASH!

All-talk radio...

SMASH!

Zombies, ninjas, pirates!

I am a robot. I like to...

SMASH! SMASH! SMASH!

+100
+200
+50
+50
+200

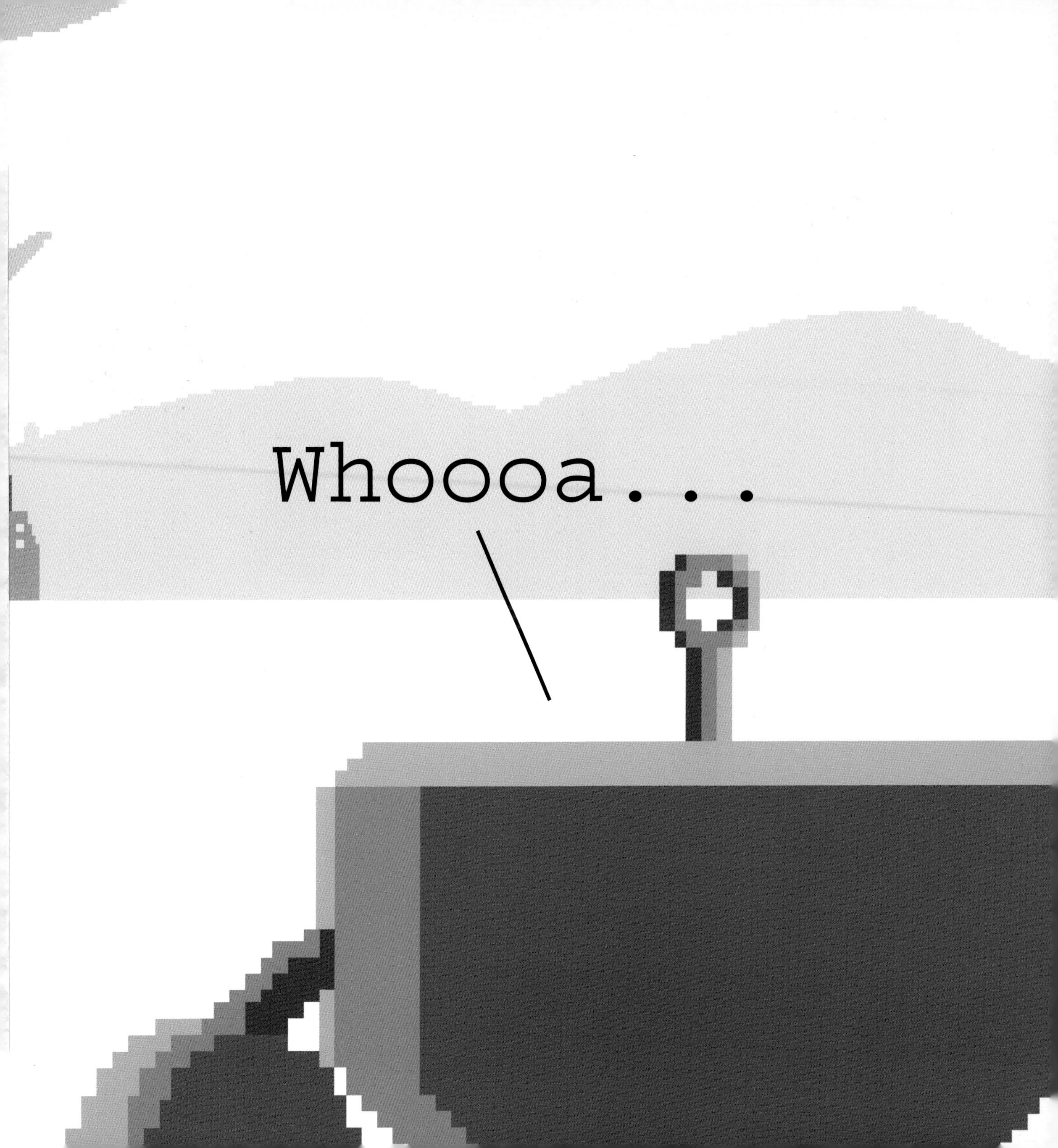
Whoooa...

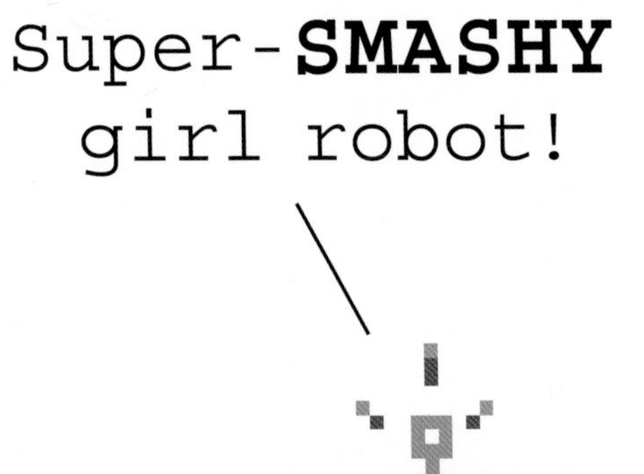
Super-**SMASHY**
girl robot!

I am a robot...

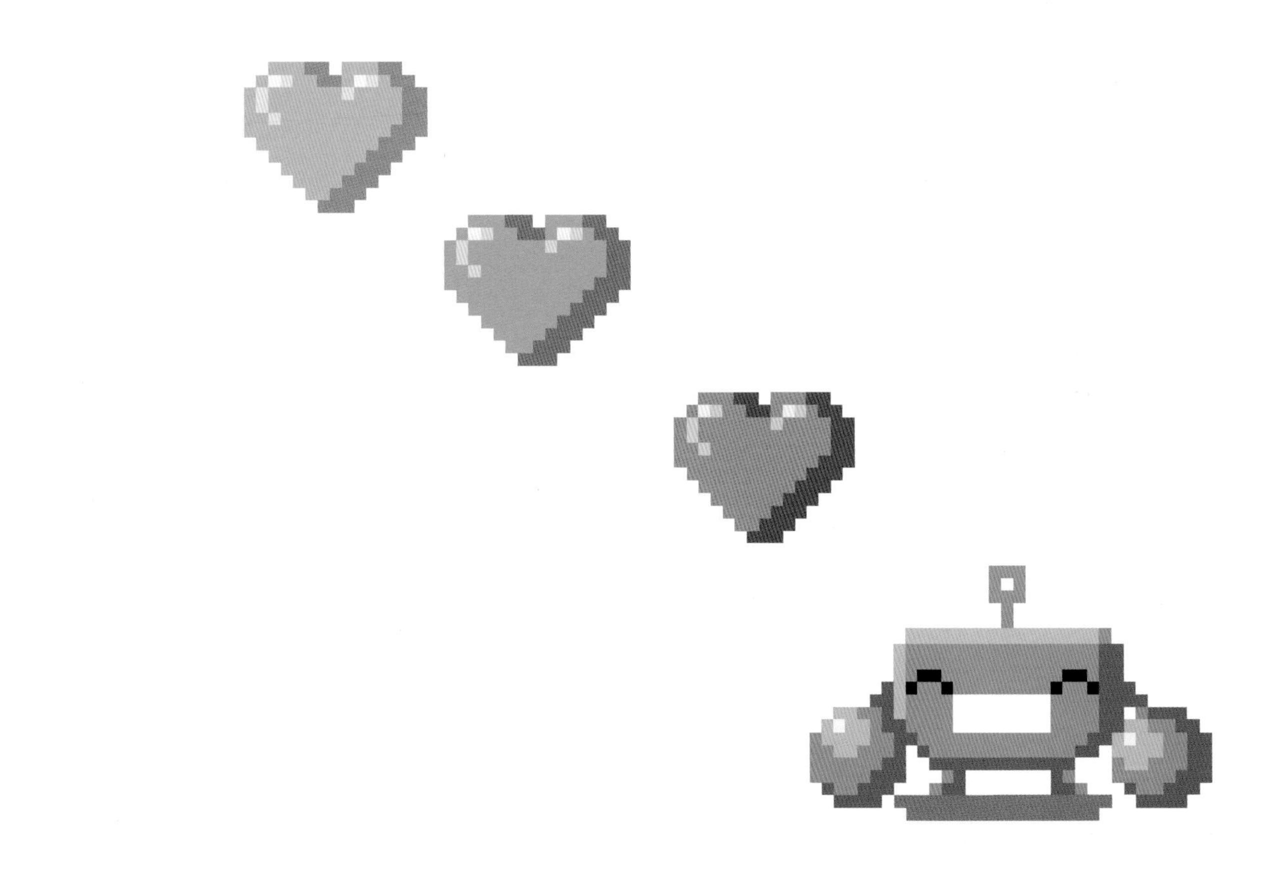

I like to...

SMASH!

I am a robot.

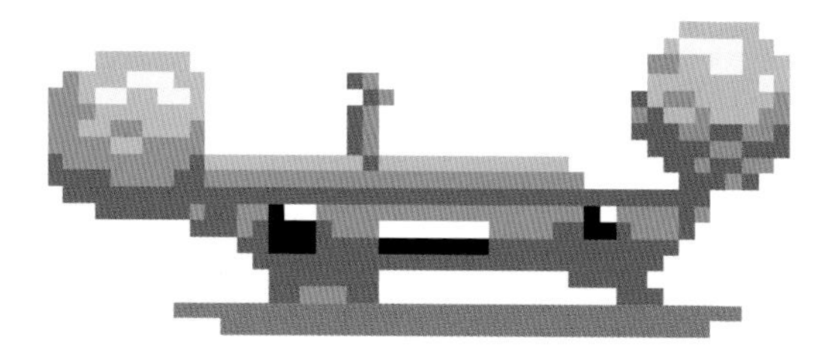

I like to...

SMASH!